Worm Story

Holt, Rinehart and Winston · New York

Worm Story

by Robert Tallon

10 9 8 7 6 5 4 3 2 1

Library of Congress Cataloging in Publication Data

Tallon, Robert, 1939-
  Worm story.

  SUMMARY: When Fat Bird offers to be friendly
and teach him to fly, Tiny Worm learns who his
true friends are.
  [1. Worms—Fiction. 2. Friendship—Fiction]
I. Title.   PZ7.T157Wo   [E]   77-10709
ISBN 0-03-021536-6

To the sweet memory of
Minnie Ha Ha, Spencer, Rex and—
the best of all—Spud

Tiny Worm poked his head
out of the ground.
"Oh! To be able to fly," he said.
Fat Bird, sitting on a branch overhead,
heard him.
"Fly? That's the easiest thing in the
world to do," he said.
"But it looks so hard," said Tiny Worm.
"I could teach anyone to fly,
if I wanted to," said Fat Bird.
"I have an extra pair of wings
right up here, in my nest."
"Could you teach me how to fly?"
asked Tiny Worm.
Fat Bird hesitated.
"Well maybe," Fat Bird said. "Of course,
I couldn't teach you to fly on the ground."

"Oh, I'll go anywhere to learn how to fly,"
Tiny Worm said.
"Well...I don't know...," said Fat Bird.
"Right now I have to go pick berries
for my dinner. Besides, what have you got
to pay me with?"
Tiny thought for a moment. "I have
nothing to give," he said, "but I could
be your friend."
"Friend!" Fat Bird snorted. "I can fly
from tree to tree; I can go anyplace
I want to. I don't need friends."
"Gee, I thought everybody needed
a friend," said Tiny Worm.
"Not me!" said Fat Bird. "I don't."

"Well, anyway, thank you, Mr. Bird,"
Tiny Worm said and started to go
back down in the ground.
"Wait just a minute," Fat Bird called.
"Because I'm a nice bird, I'm going to do
something for you."
"What's that?" Tiny asked.
"I don't have time to teach one worm,"
Fat Bird said. "But if you can get
all your friends together, we could have
a flying worm class up on my branch."
"Wonderful!" Tiny said. "I'll go tell my
friends the good news."
Fat Bird's little eyes glistened in the sun.

Tiny went below to his room and told
his friends the news.
"Silly fool!" said Green Worm.
"I wouldn't go up on a branch with a bird.
Birds love to eat us."
"No, no," said Tiny. "He's a nice bird.
He said so. He eats only berries."
"Berries—with a hot worm sandwich,"
said Long Worm.
"Who wants to be a flying worm, anyhow?"
asked Yellow Worm.

The worms all agreed.
None of them wanted to be flying worms.
But Tiny was determined to fly.
"I'm going up by myself, then," he said.
"Tiny, don't go," they pleaded.
"It's too dangerous."
"Crazy worm!" Pink Worm shouted.

Fat Bird was waiting.

"Where are your friends?" he asked.

"They don't want to fly," Tiny said.

"But I do!"

"Friends? Who needs them!" said Fat Bird.

"Okay, I'm going to fly you up
to my branch."

"Oh, how beautiful it is up here!"
Tiny sang out. "I can see everything.
The flowers…The hills…"

"Yeah, yeah!" Fat Bird said.

"Nature is beautiful."

"Is that your nest?" asked Tiny.

"Yeah, that's my nest," Fat Bird answered.

"Where is the extra pair of wings?"
said Tiny.

"There isn't any extra pair of wings,
stupid worm," Fat Bird said.

"No wings?" Tiny said. "How will I fly?"

"Fly? Worms can't fly! Dogs can't fly!
Elephants can't fly! Only birds can fly!"
Fat Bird shouted.

"Fat Bird, you're a liar!" Tiny yelled.

"So what!" Fat Bird shouted. "And I also
love *wormburgers*."

"You mean you're going to eat me?"
Tiny said in horror.

"That's the story," Fat Bird said.

"Help! Help!" Tiny cried out.
Fat Bird threw Tiny into the nest.
"Ha ha ha! Where are your friends now?"
he asked. "How can they help you?
They can't fly."
Tiny trembled as he looked around
the dark nest.
"What am I going to do?" he thought.
"Nobody can help me now."

Tiny's friends saw it all from their
underground peepholes.
"Poor thing, he's Fat Bird's dinner
for sure," said Yellow Worm.
"We're his friends," said Green Worm.
"We must stop Fat Bird before it's too late.
But what can we do?"
"I have a plan that might work,"
said Old Wrinkled Worm. "Gather
round me."
Old Wrinkled Worm whispered his plan
to the others. "Bzzz bzzz bzzzzzz."

"Well," Fat Bird said, "I see your dumb friends are coming out looking for you."

"Help! I'm up here!" Tiny screamed.

"Shut up," said Fat Bird. "They can't hear you."

"Hello, Mr. Fat Bird," Old Wrinkled Worm shouted up.

"What do you want, Old Worm?" said Fat Bird.

"We can't find our friend, Tiny. Has he flown away?"

Fat Bird laughed. "Right!" he said. "He caught on fast. He was flying around after one lesson."

"Fat Bird, we have reconsidered your kind offer," said Old Worm. We'd like to start taking flying lessons, too. Right away."

Fat Bird's mouth watered. "Food for winter," he thought.

"Terrific. Now you're being smart," he said.
Fat Bird flew down, and picked up each
of the worms and brought them up to
his branch.
"Heh heh heh, I've got all your friends
out here, Tiny," Fat Bird said.
Then he reached into the nest, picked Tiny
up in his beak and dropped him on the
branch, next to Old Worm.
"Stupid, dopey worms!" Fat Bird shouted.
"You're all going to be *wormburgers*
on my winter menu!" Old Wrinkled Worm
gave the signal.
"Jump! Jump!"

And all the worms jumped on
Fat Bird's back.
Fat Bird rocked back and forth, trying to
keep his balance.
"Help! What are you doing?" he cried.
"I'll fall and crack my beak."
"Fat Bird, listen to me," Old Wrinkled
Worm said. "We're going to hang on
forever unless you fly us down."
"Okay, okay, you win," Fat Bird cried.
He spread his wings, flew the worms
down to the ground,
then quickly flew back up again.

He sat pulling out his fat tail feathers
in a fit of anger.
"Hey, Fat Bird, can you hear me?"
Tiny Worm shouted, poking his head
out of the ground.
"What do you want?" Fat Bird answered.
"Now you know what friends are for,"
said Tiny Worm. "They help you when
you're in trouble.
You know something else?"
"What! What!" Fat Bird yelled.
"Fat Bird, you need a friend."

About the Author
Robert Tallon is a successful commercial artist
in a wide variety of media, including
television. His drawings appear on the covers
of many magazines, notably, the *New Yorker*
and *Time*. His *Rhoda's Restaurant* received
the Brooklyn Art Books for Children Citation
for 1975, given by the Brooklyn Museum.

Other books by Robert Tallon

Rotten Kidphabets

Zag: A Search Through the Alphabet

Fish Story

Flea Story

About the Book
The full-color art was camera-separated for printing
by offset.
The art is pen-and-ink with watercolor.
The text was set in Bookman and the display type
in Bookman and Bookman Bold Outline.